WALT DISNEY PRODUCTIONS
presents

Chip and Dale's New Home

Random House  New York

In the back of Donald Duck's garden,
near a lake, was an old toolshed.

It was the home of two small chipmunks
named Chip and Dale.

"It may need fixing up . . ." said Chip.

". . . and it may need painting . . ."
continued Dale.

". . . but it is still home sweet home,"
they said together.

But one day Chip and Dale heard voices outside.

It was Donald Duck and his three nephews,
Huey, Louie, and Dewey.

"May we have a sailboat, Uncle Donald?"
said Huey.

"We could sail all over the lake," said Louie

"And we could have so many adventures!"
said Dewey.

"It is out of the question," said Uncle Donald.
"Sailboats cost too
much money."

"But it doesn't have to cost a lot
of money," said Huey.

"We could build one ourselves,"
said Louie.

"Just give us the lumber from that
old shed," said Dewey.

"Well," said Uncle Donald, "the shed
IS old, and we don't really use it for
anything. I don't see why you can't use
the wood to build a boat."

The next morning Huey, Louie, and Dewey
began to take down the shed.

BANG! CRASH!

They pulled out nails and knocked the boards
apart.

The noise frightened Chip and Dale.
As the walls came tumbling down, they ran
away as fast as they could.

Chip and Dale stood in the grass by a tree and watched as their home was destroyed.

"Oh, this is terrible!" said Chip.

"Yes," said Dale, "but we must try to make the best of it."

Later, when the boys had gone, Chip
and Dale made a new house among the boards that
were lying on the ground.

But day by day, as the boys worked on
their boat, there were fewer and fewer
boards left.

Soon Chip and Dale had lost their
home again.

One evening, when the boat was finally finished,
Chip and Dale went aboard to get a closer look.

"Well, it is a different kind of house," said Chip,
"but I think it will do."

"Yes indeed," said Dale. "Let's move in."

They found a cozy spot inside the cabin of the boat and moved in with their things.

Soon they were fast asleep on a comfortable coil of rope.

The next morning Donald Duck and his three nephews came down to the shore.

They were ready to sail the boat.

But first Louie painted a name on it.

They called the boat THE WILD DUCK.

No one knew that the two chipmunks were on board.

Daisy Duck came down to help name the boat.
She swung a bottle hard toward the bow.
"This is the way they name big ships,"
she said.
But she hit Donald Duck's head instead
of the boat.

For a minute,
he did not know
where he was.

Meanwhile Daisy and the boys climbed
into the boat.

"Wait for me!" cried Donald.

He climbed a rope to get into the boat.

When the boat started to move, Chip
and Dale woke up.

"Help! What's happening?" they cried.

They ran up on deck.

"We are out on the lake!" said Chip.

Nobody saw Chip and Dale.
The boys were busy with the sail.
Daisy steered the boat.
And Donald Duck gave orders to
the crew.

"It is fun to sail," said Chip.

"But we need sailor suits," said Dale.

So when no one was looking, they cut some cloth out of the sail.

Then they each made a fine sailor suit.

When Donald Duck saw the holes in the sail,
he was furious.

"We have stowaways on board!" he shouted.
"Wait until I get my hands on them!"

Chip and Dale were afraid.
They ran down into the cabin to hide.

When they got there, they found a table
loaded with all kinds of food.

"This looks delicious!" said Chip.

"Let's eat!" said Dale.

And so they did.

Donald, Daisy, and Dewey were very angry
when they found their food had been eaten.

"This has gone too far!"
shouted Donald. "I must find
those pests."
But the two little chipmunks
had hidden again.

Not long after that a storm came up.
Big waves rocked the boat.
Daisy, Donald, and the nephews
felt very sick.
The two chipmunks were sick, too.
"We need some fresh air," said Chip.

The chipmunks found
a knothole.
"Let's try to knock it out,"
said Dale.

"One, two, three, PUSH!"

They pushed out the knothole and
water poured into the bottom of the boat.
"Let's get out of here!" shouted Chip.
"We will drown!"

The bottom of the boat was soon filled
with water.

"Help! We're sinking," shouted Huey.

He and Dewey began to scoop out the water
with buckets.

"Head for the shore," shouted Donald Duck.
Daisy steered the boat in the direction
of land.

The storm grew worse.
No one knew where they were.
Rain poured down and lightning flashed.
The waves got higher.
Suddenly one of the waves pushed the boat
up on shore.

"Let's turn the boat over," said Donald,
"so we can get out of the rain. When it stops,
we can find out where we are."

Huey, Louie, and Dewey helped push
the boat over.

By this time they were all very tired,
so they crawled under the boat and curled up
to take a nap.

But Chip and Dale
did not fall asleep.
They were angry.
"I have had enough
of this boat," said Chip.

"Yes," said Dale. "I do not want to be
a sailor."

Then they started to break up the boat.
They kicked it and broke off pieces.

And then they pulled all the nails out.

Donald, Daisy, and the nephews woke up
the next morning and crawled out from under
the boat.

When they looked around, they were
happy to see that they were home!

"THE WILD DUCK is a good boat,"
said Donald. "It has brought us right back
home where we started from."

He patted the bottom of the boat.

BANG! CRASH! The whole thing fell down
around his head, because the chipmunks
had taken out all the nails.

Huey, Louie, and Dewey could not help laughing.

But then they said, "Don't worry, Uncle Donald. We were tired of sailing anyway. We will build you a new shed with the wood."

"Well, there is plenty of it," said Donald.

So Huey, Louie, and Dewey started working
right away.

They built a fine new shed right where
the old one had been.

When they were finished, they painted it
bright red.

It was a beautiful shed, with new windows
and a new door.

As soon as it was finished, Chip and Dale moved in with their things.

"At last we are back in our home sweet home," said Chip.

"And doesn't everything look nice?" said Dale.

But several days later Chip and Dale
looked out the window and saw Huey, Louie,
and Dewey coming toward the shed carrying their
tools.

"I think the wood from the shed will
make a fine spaceship," said Louie.

"Oh, no!" said Dale. "Here we go again!"